little loon

Fran Hodgkins

Illustrated by Karel Hayes

The artwork in this book is dedicated to my in-laws, Pauline and Jay Gorey, who purchased a cottage on Wakondah Pond over thirty years ago and who were the first to introduce me to loons. I'd also like to thank my friends Phyllis and Jordan Prouty for all their efforts for the preservation of loons.

— Karel Hayes

Down East Books

Published by Down East Books
A wholly owned subsidary of The Rowman & Littlefield Publishing Group, Inc.
4501 Forbes Boulevard, Suite 200, Lanham, Maryland 20706
www.rowman.com

Unit A, Whitacre Mews, 26-34 Stannary Street, London SE11 4AB

Distributed by NATIONAL BOOK NETWORK

Text copyright © 2015 by Fran Hodgkins
Illustrations copyright © 2015 by Karel Hayes

Library of Congress Cataloging in Publication data:
Hodgkins, Fran, 1964-
    Little loon / Fran Hodgkins ; illustrated by Karel Hayes.
        pages cm
    ISBN 978-1-60893-372-3 (cloth : alk. paper) -- ISBN 978-1-60893-373-0 (electronic) 1. Loons--Juvenile literature.
I. Hayes, Karel, 1949- illustrator. II. Title.
    QL696.G33H63 2015
    598.4'42--dc23
                                        2015011210

♾™ The paper used in this publication meets the minimum requirements of American National Standard for Information Sciences—Permanence of Paper for Printed Library Materials, ANSI/NISO Z39.48-1992.

Printed in the United States

The female loon soared over the lake. She scanned the water below with her ruby-red eyes. She didn't see her mate, but she heard his distinctive call.

DID YOU KNOW?

Scientists think loons' distinctive red eyes help them see underwater.

She followed the sound and soon splashed down next to him. The loons greeted each other; they had spent a long winter apart. But their greeting was interrupted by another sound.

Thwack! Thwack! Thwack! It was the sound of a hammer on wood. The loons had never heard it here on their lake before.

On the shore, near where they nested, stood the wooden frame of a cabin. A dock jutted out into the water. A boat bobbed next to the dock.

The loons watched the activity. They could smell the scent of the people and they slowly paddled away. They would need a new place to nest. Their old nest had been right where the dock now was.

They needed a place where their eggs would be safe. The water couldn't be too close, or it might wash away the eggs. It couldn't be too far, either, because the loons couldn't walk on land very well.

It took a couple of days, but they found a good spot on a little island. Together they built a nest. The female settled in. She laid one olive brown egg with darker brown spots.

Once the egg was laid, both loons took turns sitting on it.

After nearly a month, the chick started calling to her parents from inside the egg

With a lot of work, the little loon broke out of the egg. The male loon took the eggshell and sank it in the lake away from the nest. The female stayed with their brown, fuzzy chick.

Less than a day after hatching, the little loon joined her parents in the water. Together, the loon family swam away; they didn't need the nest anymore.

The little loon soon became a good swimmer. When she got tired, she clambered onto her mother's or father's back for a snooze.

They usually spent less than a minute under water. Their big feet propelled them quickly along, and their sharp eyes spied small perch, minnows, and little sunfish that were just the right size for their chick.

But the chick couldn't catch fish. The down that kept her warm also kept her afloat. When she tried to dive, she popped back up like a cork.

LOOK AND LISTEN

Loons are larger than ducks but smaller than geese.

They have a lean, pointed shape with a distinctive checkerboard pattern of black and white and a white "necklace" around their throats.

Their haunting cries can be both soothing and unnerving. The cry is the loon's way of saying, "I'm here. Where are you?"

So her parents caught fish for her to eat.

Three weeks after the chick hatched, gray feathers replaced her fuzzy down. Now, she could dive like her parents.

Over the summer, the loons ate lots of fish — nearly half a ton's worth! On all that good fish, the young loon grew quickly. White scallops appeared on her back, and the beginnings of a white necklace, just like those her parents wore, encircled her throat.

Summer wore away and fall came. The man who owned the cabin closed it up tight for the winter. The loon family watched with interest. They, too, were preparing for winter. The young loon watched her mother and father take off by racing across the lake and rising into the sky.

DID YOU KNOW?

Loons are one of the few species of bird with solid bones, which help them dive as deep as 250 feet.

But solid bones are not so helpful for flying. Loons need a "runway" of at least 100 feet in order to build up enough speed for takeoff.

She flapped her wings in excitement, eager to follow. As she flapped them, her wings grew stronger. Before the leaves fell, the young loon was big enough and strong enough to fly.

One morning, her parents took off from the lake. They were beginning their migration to the sea, where they would spend the winter. The young loon stayed behind. She would follow her parents soon, but for now she was content to paddle about and dive for fish.

One afternoon, when all the leaves had fallen from the trees, the young loon paddled to one of her favorite fishing spots.

A sunken log attracted many minnows to its safe nooks and crannies. The loon had been here with her parents, and she knew that good food lay beneath the surface.

But something else lurked there, too.

The young loon dove and quickly caught a sunfish. When she surfaced, she felt a tug on her leg. When she tried to kick, she couldn't move. She flapped her wings and cried out in alarm.

The loon was caught by a coil of fishing line. A week earlier, the man who owned the cabin had been fishing. His line had snagged on the fallen tree, and he had cut it. The clear nylon line was nearly invisible in the water.

The loon struggled and splashed.

Across the lake, two people saw the frantic loon through binoculars. They realized she was in trouble, so they paddled their kayaks toward the struggling young bird.

The woman and man were at the lake to count the loons. All over the state, people were visiting lakes to find out how many loons lived at each one. They had been very happy to see the young loon.

The loon watched the kayaks approach. She splashed and flapped and kicked. Trapped by the fishing line, she could not escape.

The kayaks drifted close and the man reached over and gently caught the loon.

"It's her leg!" he said, lifting the startled loon out of the water. Now the bird could see something shiny and thin tangled around her left leg.

The woman leaned over and grasped her leg. The loon kicked but the woman held on tight. With a pocket knife, she cut the line. As soon as it fell away, the man let the loon go.

The young loon sped across the lake, wings flapping, and rose into the air. She circled around and saw the people sitting next to each other, looking at something shiny. The lost fishing lure. The woman wrapped up the lure and stowed it in her kayak.

The loon circled her home lake one more time. The autumn light and cool air told her it was time to go, time to find another lake, where other young loons were gathering. Then together they would make their first trip to the sea.

The loon turned south, away from the only home she had known. In a few years, she would be back, to find her own mate and raise her own chicks, just like her parents before her.

The End

WHAT CAN YOU DO?

The most dangerous predator to loons is man. Human activities, like boating and fishing, threaten loons. They may become entangled in fishing line and drown, or swallow fishing weights or lead shot and become poisoned. The presence of a boat nearby may make a loon so nervous that she leaves the nest and stops incubating the eggs. People in powerboats can injure or even kill the birds without ever realizing they are there, and the boat's wake can flood a nest and destroy the eggs. Building cabins, homes, and resorts at lakes where loons nest can make them abandon a nest they have used for years.

If you are lucky enough to find a loon nest, don't go near it, and don't stay nearby for too long. The best way to watch loons is from a distance. And if you go camping on a lake or pond in the summer, you may get to hear their beautiful and eerie calls at night and in the early morning.